My Favorite Memories

Blue Dot Kids Press
www.BlueDotKidsPress.com

Original English-language edition published in 2020 by Blue Dot Kids Press, PO Box 2344,
San Francisco, CA 94126. Blue Dot Kids Press is a trademark of Blue Dot Publications LLC.

Original English-language edition © 2020 Blue Dot Publications LLC
Original English-language edition translation © 2020 Elisabeth Lauffer

German-language edition originally published in Germany under the title *Meine liebsten Dinge
müssen mit* © 2018 by Beltz & Gelberg, in the publishing group Beltz-Weinheim Basel

This English-language translation is published under exclusive license with Beltz & Gelberg
Original English-language edition designed by Susan Szecsi

To request permissions or to order copies of this publication, contact the publisher at
www.BlueDotKidsPress.com.

Cataloging in Publication Data is available from the United States Library of Congress.
ISBN: 978-1-7331212-4-8

Printed in China with soy inks.
First Printing

Sepideh Sarihi   Julie Völk

MY FAVORITE
MEMORIES

BLUE DOT KIDS PRESS

I was brushing my hair when Papa
came in and told me we were moving.
Mama was very excited. Papa too.

"We'll fly in an airplane to another country and
live in a new house there," said Papa.

They gave me a new suitcase, so I could pack. Mama said I could only take my most favorite things.

I had an aquarium. It was one of my
favorite things.

I had a wooden chair that my grandpa
had made for me. It was one of my
favorite things too.

We had a pear tree outside our house that
was the exact same age as me. But that was
too big to pack, of course. It was another
one of my favorite things, though.

I liked our bus driver because he always sang songs with us. I wanted to take him and our school bus too. They were some of my favorite things.

Oh, I almost forgot:

my friend! My best friend! She was always
such a good listener.

I went to Mama and said, "The suitcase
is too small. Can I have a bigger one?"

"No, there's not much room in the airplane.
We all have to take small suitcases."

I told Mama that, in that case, I couldn't come.
Then I sadly walked down to the ocean. The ocean
was also one of my favorite things.

But that was something I didn't have to take with me.

That's the great thing about the ocean—it's everywhere.

Then I had an idea!

Here in our new home, we don't live as close to the ocean.

Papa gave me a bike,
so I can ride to the shore every day.

I'm still waiting for the bottles with
my most favorite things inside.

For my aquarium, for my friend, for the
school bus and driver, for my wooden chair,
and for my pear tree.

I know it might take a little while.
But that's okay—I can wait.

Sepideh Sarihi was born in 1988 in Iran.
She studied screenwriting and dramaturgy in
Tehran, where she later worked for various
magazines and in children's television. She has
lived in Germany since 2012 and is studying
fine art at the Bauhaus University, Weimar.

Julie Völk was born in Vienna, Austria, and studied at the Hamburg University of Applied Sciences. She lives with her family near Vienna. Her picture books have won many awards, including the White Raven Award from the International Youth Library.